WELCOME TO
PASSPORT TO READING
A beginning reader's ticket to a brand-new world!

Every book in this program is designed to build read-along and read-alone skills, level by level, through engaging and enriching stories. As the reader turns each page, he or she will become more confident with new vocabulary, sight words, and comprehension.

These PASSPORT TO READING levels will help you choose the perfect book for every reader.

READING TOGETHER
Read short words in simple sentence structures together to begin a reader's journey.

READING OUT LOUD
Encourage developing readers to sound out words in more complex stories with simple vocabulary.

READING INDEPENDENTLY
Newly independent readers gain confidence reading more complex sentences with higher word counts.

READY TO READ MORE
Readers prepare for chapter books with fewer illustrations and longer paragraphs.

This book features sight words from the educator-supported Dolch Sight Words List. This encourages the reader to recognize commonly used vocabulary words, increasing reading speed and fluency.

For more information, please visit www.passporttoreadingbooks.com.

Enjoy the journey!

Little, Brown and Company

Hachette Book Group
1290 Avenue of the Americas, New York, NY 10104
Visit our website at www.lb-kids.com

Little, Brown and Company is a division of Hachette Book Group, Inc.
The Little, Brown name and logo are trademarks of Hachette Book Group, Inc.

The publisher is not responsible for websites (or their content)
that are not owned by the publisher.

First Edition: October 2013

Library of Congress Cataloging-in-Publication Data

Jakobs, D. (Devlan), 1974–
Holly, jolly harmony / adapted by D. Jakobs ; based on the episode "Hearth's Warming Eve" written by Merriwether Williams. — First edition.
pages cm. — (My little pony) (Passport to reading. Level 2)
ISBN 978-0-316-22816-9
I. Williams, Merriwether. Hearth's warming eve. II. Title.
PZ7.J1535545Hol 2013
[E]—dc23
2013007284

10 9 8 7 6 5 4

CW

Printed in the United States of America

Passport to Reading titles are leveled by independent reviewers applying the standards developed by Irene Fountas and Gay Su Pinnell in *Matching Books to Readers: Using Leveled Books in Guided Reading*, Heinemann, 1999.

LICENSED BY:

HOLLY, JOLLY HARMONY

Adapted by **D. Jakobs**

Based on the episode "Hearth's Warming Eve"

written by **Merriwether Williams**

LITTLE, BROWN AND COMPANY

New York Boston

Attention, My Little Pony fans!
Look for these items when you read this book.
Can you spot them all?

wreath

tree

food

Windigo

The pony friends love the holiday
called Hearth's Warming Eve.
It is a time of harmony and friendship.

The ponies of Canterlot
decorate each wreath and tree
with stars, bells, and ribbons.
The city looks so pretty!

Each year,

the ponies and Spike put on a show.

The ponies play different parts

while Spike tells the story.

Once, there were three pony tribes.

The leaders of the Earth Ponies, the Pegasi,

and the Unicorns were named

Chancellor Puddinghead,

Commander Hurricane, and Princess Platinum.

The Pegasi made the weather.

The Earth Ponies grew the food.

The Unicorns used magic
to make day and night.

This was not a happy time.

The three tribes did not get along.

Then one day a huge snowstorm

stopped the crops from growing.

Everypony was running out of food!

The three tribe leaders blamed one another.

The meaner they were,

the harder it snowed.

Each leader decided to find a new land for her tribe.

Private Pansy went with
Commander Hurricane.
Flying in the snowstorm
was scary.

Princess Platinum was glad
to leave the others.
"Do you agree?"
she asked Clover the Clever.
"We could have tried harder,"
Clover answered.

Smart Cookie and Chancellor Puddinghead
kept getting lost.
Puddinghead might have been using
her map wrong.

All the ponies found new homes
for their tribes.

"I name this land Pegasopolis,"
said Hurricane.

"I am double-dazzled
by all these jewels,"
said Princess Platinum.
"I name this land Unicornia!"

"This dirt is the dirtiest!
I name this land Dirtville!"
said a happy Puddinghead.
"How about we call it Earth?"
asked Smart Cookie.

But each tribe leader had
chosen the same land!
"I planted my flag first!"
"Did not!"
"Did too!" they argued.

As the pony leaders yelled,
snow and winds appeared.
"Oh no!" said Hurricane.
"Not again!"

Instead of beautiful,
it was blizzardy.
Instead of wonderful,
it was wintry.
Instead of spectacular,
it was snow-tacular.

The ponies needed a safe place to hide from the storm.
The only shelter was a cave.

"Earth Ponies are fools!"
said Hurricane.

"Unicorns are snobs!"
said Puddinghead.

"Pegasi are brutes!"
said Platinum.

When the pony leaders called
one another mean names,
they were frozen in ice.

The other ponies heard wails
coming from outside the cave.
"It is a Windigo!" said Clover.
"A Windigo is a winter spirit
who feeds on hate.
It froze our leaders!"

"I do not hate you," said Pansy.

"Me neither," Clover agreed.

"It does not matter if we are different. We are all ponies!" said Cookie.

A pinkish-purple heart burst
from Clover's horn.
It chased away the Windigo.
The ice began to melt.

"This magic came from
all three of us," said Clover.
"We joined together in friendship!"

All three tribes became friends.
They sang songs that became
the winter carols everypony
still sings today.

Ponies have been kind
to one another ever since.
Together, they named
their new land Equestria!
And that is the story
of Hearth's Warming Eve.